# FOUR STAGES

## CHRONICLES OF SWORDSFALL™

### BY

### BRANDON DIXON

Copyright © 2019 by Swordsfall Studios LLC.

All rights reserved. This book or any portion thereof may not be reproduced or used in any manner whatsoever without the express written permission of the publisher except for the use of brief quotations in a book review.

Xavian Illustration by Chris Cold

Door Photo by Denny Muller

Cover Design by Brandon Dixon

Written by Brandon Dixon

Printed in the United States of America

https://www.swordsfall.com/

CHRONICLES OF SWORDSFALL

FOUR STAGES

*Content Warning*

**This story deals with Alcoholism and shades of domestic abuse and implied violence**

# INTRODUCTION

*A Spirit Medium from an elite division known as The Eyes of Garuda was commissioned to help in the investigation of a grisly quadruple homicide. The investigators assigned were baffled by the case. What they uncovered during the Mediums vision would change everything.*

*This vision would give the first glimpse into Xavian's Touch, a deadly mixture of curse and disease that links the victim to The Withering King himself, Xavian.*

*The following is a re-telling of what the Medium saw that fateful day.*

**The Four Stages of Xavian's Touch**

- Stage 1 - Infection
- Stage 2 - Host Preparation
- Stage 3 - Mental Degradation
- Stage 4 – The Invitation

# INCUBATION

"They don't even know what they've LOST!"

The man bellowed as he haphazardly kicked a small branch that had dared to cross his path. He balled his hands, the can crushing between them. His jawline clenched with indignation as his brain replayed the day. The soft crunch of his shoes against the damp leaves echoed as he slogged his way home. Life in the evergreen of the Ilun Valley wasn't always easy and the weather was as fickle as it was docile. For men like him working on a large crop-share was the best way to ride out the unproductive post-harvest months. Though even in such a prosperous industry, some jobs were undoubtedly better than others. That was the kind of job this man had. Well, formerly had until an impromptu conversation with the crotchety crop-owner, Sochalla.

The man's caring but slightly prying partner, Danil, had begged him emphatically to cut back on the drinking. She didn't understand how relieved the man had felt to find himself on easy street finally. Sochalla's crop-share was painless work for great pay. So why not celebrate after the hard run of luck they had had?

You only have one mortal body, may as well enjoy it, right?

And oh, how he had enjoyed it.

As had Danil. The young, beautiful couple had little problems finding a place to live in the Valley once they had decided on it. It was Danil's eagle eye that had found the diamond in the rough they now call home. They were *finally* in the right place at the right time. He had the right job, the right partner. There was nowhere for him to go but up. Nowhere.

So, when the old boss Sochalla pulled the man over for a private chat, he thought it was for his long-overdue raise. Instead, the slender, silver-haired owner brought up the man's, as he called it "drinking habit". Then began accusing the man of having alcohol on his breath at the beginning of shift every morning.

The man, as an upstanding citizen, of course, denied the charges. A few drinks at night in the privacy of your own home didn't count as a *problem*. Sochalla disagreed, and after a tense back and forth the man left the crop-share unemployed. Leaving with seemingly only his pride.

The man threw the mangled remains of the can into the public trash can he was walking past. The early afternoon sun glancing off of the can as it landed.

So now here the man was, walking home, trying to figure out how to explain this injustice to his partner. Knowing her, she'd tell him to go pray at the Ishvana's shrine tucked behind the town hall. He didn't believe in divine intervention and she knew it. Nor had he ever been interested in it either. The man had seen enough awful things happen to good people to know that prayers alone did little. As far as he was concerned both The Divinity and The Divine Order were useless for common people like him.

From their vaulted positions, how could they possibly understand his life? His STRUGGLES? How could he trust beings whose smile never seemed to change? The corners of their mouths perfectly unmarked by time. Small broken pieces of time that pretended to be one of us. Walking sticks of dust like Sochalla were just playing for sympathy in the eyes of the deities. If only...

What, where was he?

The man's thoughts screeched to a halt as he stopped in minor confusion. Some combination of pent-up anger and his worries had diverted his attention, for he had arrived at his doorstep on autopilot. The man chided himself for being so deep in thought as to walk all the way home and not even realize it. The man's breathe fogged in front of him as he exhaled.

Trying to relax, he reflexively rubbed his sore jaw. The stress had had him clenching his jaw all the way home, chewing on it like jerky. If he could just make it through tonight it would be ok. In the morning he'd sit down and find a different crop-share to work. Jobs like that were a dime a dozen.

Everything would be perfectly alright. Right?

# STAGE ONE

The door trembled was fury as it was slammed shut. The man was storming out of the house in a small fit of rage of now.

"She just didn't seem to understand at all!"

He had thought that maybe Danil would get it just a little bit after all this time. His partner hadn't even given pause to the current comfort of their life. Hadn't given pause to the tiresome work he had put in to get them here, to THIS very place. It wasn't easy to stay in this part of the Valley after all. Plenty of other young couples would absolutely *KILL* to have live in this location.

The man knew how important it was to live here in this part of the valley. The status it portrayed as well as the expectations that come with living in the Ilun Valley. Of course, the man knew these things, he was the one who had found it after all.

The conversation had somehow gone worse than even he had imagined possible. He had foolishly forgotten Danil was close with the partner of one of the other crophands. Danil had been ready for him before he had even stepped inside the house. She had been incorrigible that he had been fired over being drunk at the job.

The man had tried to explain to her he was just as shocked, but the words didn't come out right when he said it. She had even accused him of being drunk right then and there! The man had been shocked, after all the years they spent together he figured she'd remember how high his limit was. He tried to remind her, but that just made it worse. Why couldn't she just see it from his viewpoint?

*Why is she never on your side?*

The harsh evening wind blew across him. He shivered as the thought seemed to invade his mind. She never really was on his side now that he thought about it. It was like Danil always listening to her mother or her friends, or his friends, or his neighbors. But Danil never seemed listened to him though.

He gazed up at the setting evening sky, it's burgundy hue slowly retreating below the treeline. His favorite hangout should be open by now, the man thought to himself with a self-serving nod.

It was the one place he could go to for total solace. A place he could be *him*, and no one would judge him. The one place where he could be understood and the people understood him. Especially the owner. They were the best of mates.

*You don't need anyone.*

And maybe it was best that way actually. Plenty of people would agree with that through, right? The man knew some people who definitely think that. Especially the tavern owner, um...

The man couldn't remember the name of the tavern owner at the moment. But he knew he liked them. It always seemed as if no matter what the man ordered, the drink would be stiff as a somber tree.

A pause.

The small sign of the tavern was just in front of him. Was the walk always that short? The man shook his head, scattering the thoughts wayward. The stress from how everyone had done him wrong today had him phasing through life.

As the man usually did, he told the owner to serve him up something especially loud. There was a wordless, stiff nod and a curt turn as the tavern owner set to make his drink.

"When I say loud, I mean LOUDER than my WIFE."

The man chuckled at his own lazy attempt at humor. The greying, unnamed tavern owner stared at the man for a moment then continued making the drink. Letting the feeble joke fall flat. The man stared beams at the top of the owner's head for a moment. The swishing sound of ice and liquor mixing only added to the dead air.

Maybe the man didn't like the tavern owner as much as he thought he had.

**He doesn't care either.**

The man glared at the barkeep as his first drink of the evening was delivered. Before the barkeep could even properly introduce the drink, the man had grabbed it and in one crisp motion, gulped the shot down. He slammed the empty glass down on the wood countertop, leaned back and punctuated the air with a loud burp.

"Ahhh, that hit the spot right there. I remember why I used to like you now."

The owner reeled back a bit from the brash phrasing, their mouth turning downwards. The man pushed the glass forward, motioning for another one with a hurried motion.

"One more time, barkeep."

"I think you've had more than enough, friend, " an overly sweet smile pressed to the owner's face as they spat out the words.

The man glared silently at the bar owner for a moment. Shocked by the well-deserved retort, glancing left and right to see if anyone else was hearing this.

"Um, excuse me? I just got here? It's a little early to be cutting me off don't you think?"

The barkeeper met the man's glare with an inquisitive look. The aging owner motioned to the left of the man. A small stack of nine drink glasses sat to the side of the counter, lined up and stacked like a pyramid. The man was pleased to see someone else also appreciated a triangle of finished drinks.

"If you don't remember the other drinks you've had, then its definitely time for you to leave," the owner said definitively. Returning the liquor bottle to below the counter. The man stared vacantly at the unwashed glassware.

Were those his?

When had he ordered those?

Maybe the barkeep had made those drinks extra loud after all...

"Well seeing as how I don't remember them, I think that means we can start the count over." the man smiled slyly with a wink.

"Do I need to get a message to Danil?"

The man stiffened at his partner's name. There she was again, intruding his solace from afar. Why were the people around him constantly imposing their will on his life? The man began to wonder to himself. Maybe THAT'S why he didn't remember the other drinks. It was all part of some clever ploy to make him think he had been drinking too much. The man wondered to himself if Danil had had anything to do with his sudden and unwarranted termination. She had known about it awfully fast, even with her being friends with other people the crop.

*You can't trust anyone.*

He reached into his pocket pulled out a couple of azurean chips and tossed them on the counter. It was clear to him this was no longer HIS place. And if it wasn't his place, then he'd pay for his drink like a stranger. It was even more clear to him how little respect he had in this town. In this supposed ORDER.

"Don't worry, I'm done here."

The man could hear the owner call out to him as the man unsteadily stood and stumbled toward the door. The man scoffed at the cheap floorwork. The uneven surface making his exit less dramatic than he had hoped. What cheap construction he thought to himself. He could barely remember why he wasted his time coming to such a dive.

***You're better off by yourself***

Yes, the man thought, yes he was.

# STAGE TWO

The man was back on the streets again, wandering aimlessly. Listlessly. The night breeze swept leaves down the road, the air still and quiet. A striped cat sauntered into his vision. An eclectic and almost random arrangement of black and white fur. The cat stopped upon seeing the man. Glancing him up and down for a moment before slowly moving in the man's direction.

The man stared at the feline for a second, was it a feral cat looking for food perhaps? The cat sat on its back legs right in front of the man and let out a soft meow. Leaning forward to lick its shoulder for a moment, then meowing again since the first hadn't elicited a reaction.

Nope, just a normal cat.

He reached down and pet the fluffy animal. It responded with a confirming purr.

The man gently picked up the scraggly ebony and grey cat. The gentle purr of the pleased kitty reverbed through his chest. He had always connected to cats like this. They gave him this warm feeling in his chest when he was around them. The weight would lift from his shoulders. His mind free of the burdens set on him.

Unfortunately, Danil didn't share the same love of them, and the house was devoid of furry friends. A fact that didn't escape him as he found solace in the cat.

**They never let you be you.**

He nodded as he continued to nuzzle the vibrating bundle of fluff. The man smiled as he felt its wet kisses and licks. He just wanted to be himself and free. What was wrong with a drink a time or two? Who didn't need a few drinks before work? The early morning wake up time and a solemn walk to work everyday dulled the senses. A good ale just helped make it all bearable. Make all the monotony, worth, SOMETHING.

Unfortunately, life continues to be just as despondent after the rise and shine drinks gentle euphoria faded. It was for the betterment of everyone at work that he had a lunchtime shot of something steep.

It was like they were punishing him for being human. When had the world become like that? You wouldn't enjoy a relaxing furry friend in your own home? The man looked up as he slowly drifted back to reality. He glanced around at his surroundings in a daze, he had wandered almost to the edge of their town. The paved road gave way to a dirt one that ended at the wall of endless trees that was the Kanil Forest to the west.

And there was nothing in those forests for a human at night.

The man sighed, he had nothing else to do at this point really. He kicked at the dirt, spending bits it the air with a huff. It was time for him to just head back home.

***If you had power, things would be different.***

A crisp night wind racked across his body provoking another shiver. Yea. That's right. It wasn't just time for him to go home, it was time for him to go and *take* his life back. To find his power, to not feel like a passenger in his own life.

He something soft in his hand as he turned to return home.

A tan bad was clutched in his arms. Cradled.

Why had he picked this junk up? The man couldn't seem to remember and shook his head in amusement. He turned around and began walking back toward his home. The man had wandered but looky not that far. He spotted a trash pile nearby and dropped the grocery bag into it, a soft metallic jangle ringing out as it settled.

The man shook his head at his own forgetfulness. He clearly needed a drink.

# STAGE THREE

The shadows flickered across his path as the man approached his home. His hands had begun to ache from the night air and his body tired from the struggles of a tumultuous life. The mans hands slipped clumsily as he fumbled to open the door. The man was frustrated, this door was always giving him problems. No matter how many times he fixed it, it would become jammed again. Whoever kept breaking the door would pay gravely for it. The numbness of his hands was helping the matter. He continued to fumble with it for another second.

He paused as he saw a shadow move flicker across the side windows of his home. Who was at his home at this time of night?

**Betrayal**

With an exasperated huff, the man leaned back and swiftly kicked the door, popping it from its flimsy hitches. He was sick of this stupid door and it was just another example of his hard work wasted. All these people coming in and out of his home were constantly breaking his repairs. They did it KNOWING that he was going to have to fix it.

Just like everything else.

Just like his job.

He busted his ass day in and day out, first one in and the first one out. For years he drank to get by and no one, well hardly alone, had ever complained. They needed him and everyone knew it. That must have been why Sochalla, that penny pinching, skinny asshole, had him fired. The nerve of them! Never again would his hard work go to waste. And whoever was trespassing in HIS house would pay.

**DECEPTION.**

The man burst into the house and took a gander at his surroundings. Who else was here at this hour? The tangled sound of conversation and laughter came wafting from the common area. The man's hands rippled as he clenched them, moving slowly toward the sound.

Is this the wretched hour upon which that his "partner" sought to sow his ruin? If you could even call them that at this point. As the man walked past the family shrine the voices began to separate. A few of the voices sounded familiar. Did he know them? Was that a co-worker's voice he was hearing?

**THEY PLANNED THIS.**

Now it made sense. This was no accident. Who else would have made his occasional home remedy seem like something more? The creatin that fired him had known too much as well, how did he know? How had he known about his morning routines? Were they sharing information? How deep did the conspiracy go? Was there more to the story? What else had that stranger in his home said? How long had this been going on? Did they not expect him to come from his evening walk and find them there? *PLOTTING?*

***EVERYONE IS INVOLVED.***

As the man stepped into the light of the room, he slowly surveyed the room full of people. There in the corner of the crowded room was his partner. Looking like a fallen star. Their features even more obvious than usual. Impossibly tall, with sleek, beak-like, thin features. Like an awkwardly bent twig, almost invisible in its litheness. The interloper's scowl was even more pronounced than usual and seemed to be pushing the sides of her face out.

"Oh my god, where have you BEEN! We've been looking for you for days!" Their voice rasping, crashing on itself. Falling apart under the weight of her lies no doubt.

His eyes swept across the room, for one set of treacherous eyes to the next. The beloved owner of the forced labor camp that practically begged people like him to work there. He saw the flab bulbous corrupt businessman for what he really was at that moment.

Not a loving pillar of the community or stand up boss. No, he was just another leech getting plump for his hard work. The man was glad he had quit that awful crop dust of a job. They didn't deserve him anyway, especially as he could literally see his boss getting fat from his hardwork.

***FAT FROM YOUR SUCCESS.***

The man couldn't bottle up his indignation anymore. He grabbed his former boss by the collar of his neck and wrenched him forward. He leaned closer until the two of them were within spitting distance of each other. The man was going to make sure this swindler would get the message this time.

"Listen here you fat *fuck*. How dare you show your face in MY home. How long have you been planning this? I bet YOU'RE the one with the drinking problem actually. That's how you knew so much about drinking. Am I getting set up to the heat off of YOU?!"

**LOOK AT THEM ALL.**

The chorus of gasps rang throughout the room hitting the man's ears with glee as he gazed up to see the other interlopers.

Look at them.

A motley, ragtag group of saboteurs who had plotted to keep him from achieving what he was owed. What he had always *deserved*. The owner of that dive in town, someone from his work, that nosy person across the street. All of them staring at him, mouths hanging down to their knees like wet dough. They couldn't believe he had figured out their trick.

**THEY'RE ALL LIARS.**

"What the hell! You HIT Sochalla! What is wrong with you…! You storm out and don't come back for DAYS then assault that frail old man like that? …? What is wrong with you!"

The person that was his once his partner was screaming in his direction The words were almost not real. He mentally tuned them out as he knew all of it, he knew what lines they were going to spew out. After all, they wanted, they needed ALL his power. He had never really even wanted this house actually. The man didn't even love where they lived. He worked all day long, tirelessly at an Order sanctioned labor mill to provide the fake life they both led.

**DON'T LET THEM LIE TO YOU ANYMORE!**

The man struck the fat, blubbering, drunken, weak and greedy slumlord in the face again. He finally felt like he was getting somewhere. The man took a deep breath as he took in his first lungful of freedom.

**THIS IS TAKING BACK YOUR POWER!**

"YES IT IS!" his fist came crashing down into the man's face again.

TAKE MORE OF YOUR POWER BACK

"HAHAHAHAHA YES! I'LL TAKE ALL OF IT BACK!"

The man started laughing as he felt himself gaining power with each crunch. The room was filled with voices like background noise. Someone was calling a name he felt like he once knew. It barely mattered anymore. The sound of the dull thuds of his fist drowned it all out. The rage was blissful, and the revenge was sweet. The drumming of his fist matched his heartbeat.

He had found his answer.

# STAGE FOUR

The man realized that the only way for him to be whole again was to get back everything he had once lost. His time, his energy, his freedom. To do whatever he wanted, whenever he wanted. Why had he let anyone control him in the first place? The man felt a gripping touch on his shoulder, he glanced to his left to see a desiccated hand grabbing his shoulder. It's long, talon-like digits digging into his skin.

**THEY'RE TRYING TO STOP YOU.**

"NO one will stop me ever again!"

The man spun around, throwing his fist out to connect with the saboteur in his home. A meaty thud rang out as it impacted. His vision glimmered. What he was seeing was hard to understand, something didn't look right. And yet.

Heartwrenching sobs hit his ears as he strained to see with clarity, to see what entity had grasped him. A familiar person was half-collapsed against the wall, the paintings that hung on them were strewn against the floor. Tears and distraught was painted on their face.

What might have once been a table was shattered. Reduced into jangled pieces. A thinning and frail-looking man was slumped in a patterned chair on the other end of the room. His face in ruins, the patterns of their shirt washed away with blood.

"Why are you doing this Avell?" the words were soft, and strained, edged in pain. Words that made the man pause. Pause for just one moment.

*You're FREEING yourself.*

That voice, that tone, paused his whirling mind for a moment. The man's head was a jumble, a mess of conflicting emotions. A feeling of forgetfulness mixed with rage and something else. Something...

The man's mouth smacked as his mouth opened and closed, realizing they were as parched as his vision was cloudy. The squinting of his eyes was taking their toll, a headache was rising. A pressure growing in the back of his mind. His eyes had started to hurt from the daylight peeking through the window.

Sunlight?

Wait, when had the sun come up? The man was starting to feel like something was wrong. Something *felt* wrong.

*Only the POWERLESS lose control.*

Wait. Was that his partner over there, sobbing? The blood at the corner of their delicate lips, did he do that? Had he done that to his beautiful partner? The man's hands ran through his hair as he circled in place. He was losing control, rapidly. This wasn't what he thought was going to happen.

*Only the WEAK lose sight of what they want.*

How many people had been in the room again? A chorus of faces peered back at him. He knew them, he didn't know them. Why were they here? What did it matter? They wanted something from him. They were manipulating him. Somehow. They had pushed him to edge and had lashed out. This wasn't what he had wanted. Right?

**Let me in and you'll NEVER HAVE TO FEEL THIS WAY AGAIN.**

He stumbled a bit as his feet hit something, nearly sending the man careening into the wall. The man looked down to see the tavern owner. The shock white-colored hair of theirs shimmering with rust and red colors. A color unnatural. Not of their own.

The man was having a hard time understanding what was going on. He dug his thumbs into his temple as he tried to keep his thoughts straight.

**YOU are the WEAK one.**

Is that what it was all along? Was that the problem this whole time?

"They just wanted to make sure you were ok." His partners' faint whispers punctuated with soft sobs of terror. Blood ran down the side of their face. Blood? Or tears? His chest began to ache with realization.

The man sank to his knees, running his hands across his face. His mind was hazy as he tried to understand what was going on. Reaching in his memory to try and pry from it an answer.

A wetness on his face startled him as he touched it, he paused and looked at his hands. Smeared in blood and small pieces of flesh and *other* matter.

"What...what have I done. I...I...I can fix this." Red streaks were painted onto the man's pants as he tried to smear away his guilt.

*You can't go back now. SHE HATES YOU.*

The way the man's partner was looking at him was like living confirmation. The terror on their face as palpable. Everything was gone. In this, he too had failed. It was all a failure.

The man started screaming as the bitter smell of iron and copper invaded his nose. The pigment of failure stained in his skin. Felt in the deepest part of his soul.

*They're LAUGHING at you*

A wailing sound echoed around him. Was it? Laughter seemed to echo around him.

They were all pointing him.

Laughing at him.

*You know what I am...*

What was the lie? His life? This reality? This moment? The man couldn't tell.

*Let me FREE you from your mortal bonds...*

The chorus of voices mocked him as they waved bottles of liquor in front of his face. The man pressed his hands to his ears, trying to mask the sound of his failure. It was futile.

**SAY it.**

"We can go to the elder, you're sick Avell. The drinking has done something to you. This isn't like you. We can find you help, we'll talk to a Diviner."

**SAY IT**

Even when he tried to take control, they laugh. Even when he tried to take control, he failed. The two constants. He always failed. And they always laughed. So funny to watch him topple from any height, no matter how low to the ground he already was.

He wanted to be away from it all.

From the control and games.

**SAY IT!!**

The man's screams couldn't drown out all the voices. Why couldn't they all just stop? Why couldn't it ALL JUST STOP?

**SAY. IT.**

**AND IT WILL ALL END.**

The man's voice cracks raw as his screams died out, his anger and emotion drained. Empty and hollow. Whatever he had been. This Avell, was gone. No more.

He had nothing left.

Truly.

And so, the man let the words that had clutched his throat let escape from his lips.

"Xavian."

*It was highly believed at the time that the 5$^{th}$ St Murders were connected to several other high-profile murders at the time. No evidence was found to support this.*

*The suspect was never found...*

# AUTHOR'S NOTE

That was an interesting read, wasn't it?! I'm not gonna lie, when I was going back through this and editing it, I was a little shocked at how sneakily dark the story got. There is a reason for that however, and I wanted to use this to explain a bit more about Xavian, Swordsfall and myself.

Xavian is the ultimate big bad of Swordsfall and I've never been shy about talking about that. However, this early on in the universe I don't think truly readers appreciate how bad Xavian is. Not in a moral sense (he is), but in sheer power. He's a cosmic evil, an unstoppable tide that ebbs and flows with mystery. The Withering King is an unspoken horror. The one thing everyone knows can really ruin your life completely.

His curse, Xavian's Touch, is the only way he can directly toy with humans. When humans are in their weakest mental state, when their faith in the order of the world is at its lowest, that's when Xavian can worm *just* a little into someone's mind. That's where it starts. This small voice in your head that feels like yours, but not *quite*. Saying the awful, quiet parts outloud. From the inside, Xavian plays up your fears and triggers your greatest insecurities. Those moments where you might be amicable? Yea, he pulls that fear button and makes you spoil it. It's the unseen ruiner.

Xavian is Depression.

Surprise.

An invisible hand that pulls at the corners of your soul? Edging you to do bad when you yearn to do good? Vast, and yet right next to you. Immutable, unbreakable, only manageable? Oh yea, I definitely made the biggest, baddest creature in my fictional world a corporeal form of Depression.

And that's why, in the end?

The heroes will win.

Cause we can beat that monster too.

Stay warm and bundled my friends. Till next time.

-B

# GLOSSARY OF MAJOR TERMS

Beneath It All – A separation pocket dimension where Xavian is sealed

Ether – The name for the energy that powers all life.

Garuda – The largest nation in the Northern Hemisphere. Home to The Divinity and controlled by The Divine Order of the Phoenix

Etherforce – The name for the natural occurring flow of Ether

Ilun Valley – The most populace part of Garuda with a number of cities, towns and villages nested in its various caverns, cliffs and valleys.

Ishvana – An ancient creation god that is responsible for creating Tikor and much of its life. Sacrificed herself to seal Xavian.

Hekan - The name of magic in Tikor

Raksha – Ravenous monsters created by Xavian, sealed in Beneath It All

The Divinity – The general name for all the deities of Garuda. Also, the specific name for a group of the oldest and most revered of Garuda's deities.

Vinyata – The largest nation in the Southern Hemisphere. Home to The Four Pillars and controlled by The Republic of Vinyata.

Xavian – An ancient corruption god responsible for the corruption of the Elementals. Sealed away in Beneath It all.

# ABOUT THE AUTHOR

Brandon lives in the Portland area of Oregon with his other half, Ashley. When he's not obsessed with Swordsfall, he works fruitlessly on completing his burgeoning Steam game library.

Sign up for Swordsfall's newsletter at: https://www.swordsfall.com/newsletter-signup/

Connect with Swordsfall:

WEBSITE: swordsfall.com

PATREON: patreon.com/swordsfall

TWITTER: twitter.com/swordsfall1

FACEBOOK: facebook.com/swordsfallrpg

INSTAGRAM: instagram.com/swordsfallrpg

Copyright Page

Copyright © 2019 by Swordsfall Studios LLC.

All rights reserved. This book or any portion thereof may not be reproduced or used in any manner whatsoever without the express written permission of the publisher except for the use of brief quotations in a book review.

Illustrations by T'umo Mere

Map by Brandon Dixon

Cover Design by Taylor Ruddle

Printed in the United States of America

www.swordsfall.com

Made in the USA
Middletown, DE
08 November 2020